THE PARABLE OF THE TWO NEW HOUSES

"So then, everyone who hears these words of mine and obeys them will be like a wise man who built his house on the rock. The rain poured down, the rivers flooded over, and the winds blew hard against that house. But it did not fall, because it had been built on the rock. Everyone who hears these words of mine and does not obey them will be like a foolish man who built his house on the sand. The rain poured down, the rivers flooded over, the winds blew hard against that house, and it fell. What a terrible fall that was!"

St Matthew 7, 24-27

Acknowledgment

The above quotation from The Good News Bible *is reproduced by permission of Collins Publishers.*

© LADYBIRD BOOKS LTD MCMLXXVII

All rights reserved. No part of this publication may be reproduced, stored in a retrieval system, or transmitted in any form or by any means, electronic, mechanical, photo-copying, recording or otherwise, without the prior consent of the copyright owner.

The parable of
THE TWO NEW HOUSES

retold for easy reading
by SYLVIA MANDEVILLE
illustrated by DAVID PALMER

Ladybird Books Loughborough

THE TWO NEW HOUSES

Simeon wanted to build himself a new house. "It must be a good solid house for all my children, and somewhere pleasant for my wife to live," he thought.

That evening as he and his family said their prayers, he read a verse from a psalm to them.

"Unless the Lord builds a house, the builder's work is useless."

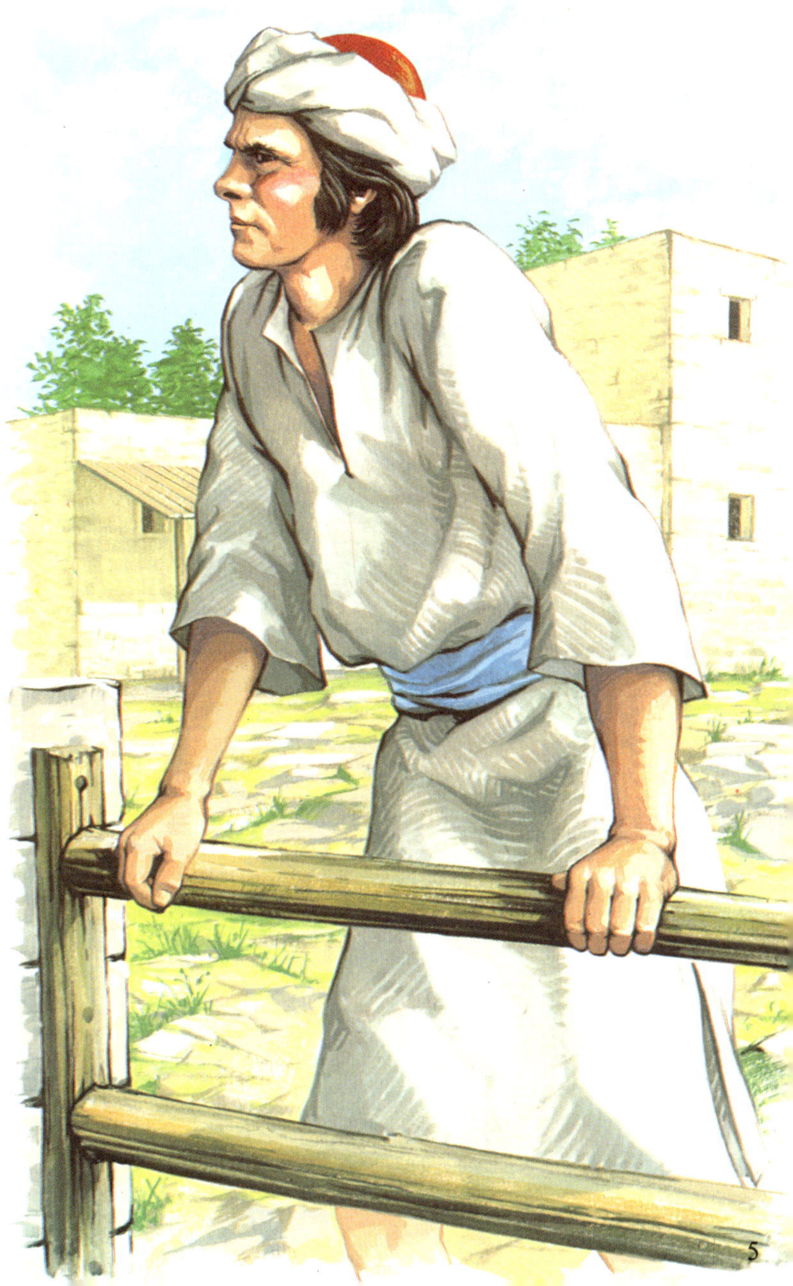

"We must think about this verse," he said. "We are going to build a big new house - we must make sure that we ask for God's help in choosing a site. We must pray that He will help the men as they build, to make the new house strong and safe."

Together the family prayed for God's help as they built their new house.

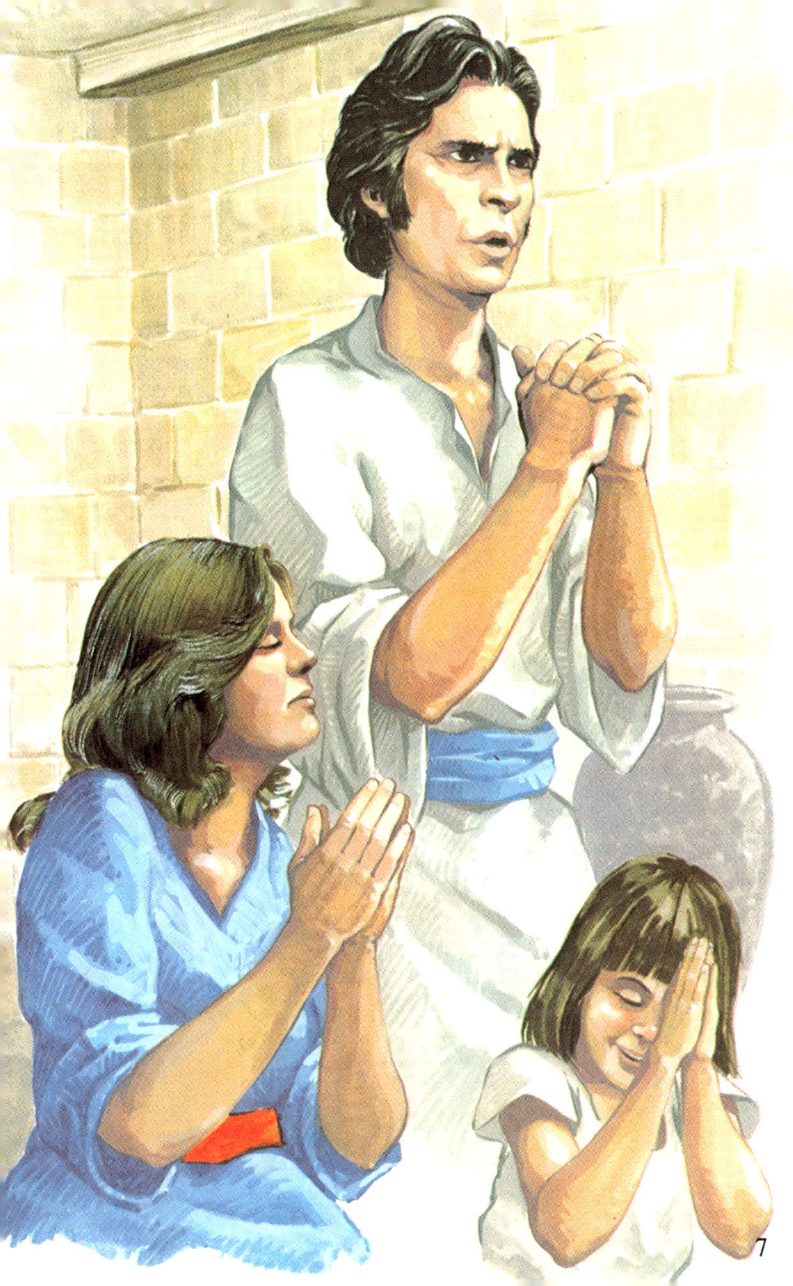

The next day, Simeon went to see a farmer who had some land to sell.

"I have plenty of land for sale, down by the river," said the farmer. "Go and have a look and see which part you want to buy."

Simeon went down to the river, praying as he went that God would help him to choose a good place to build.

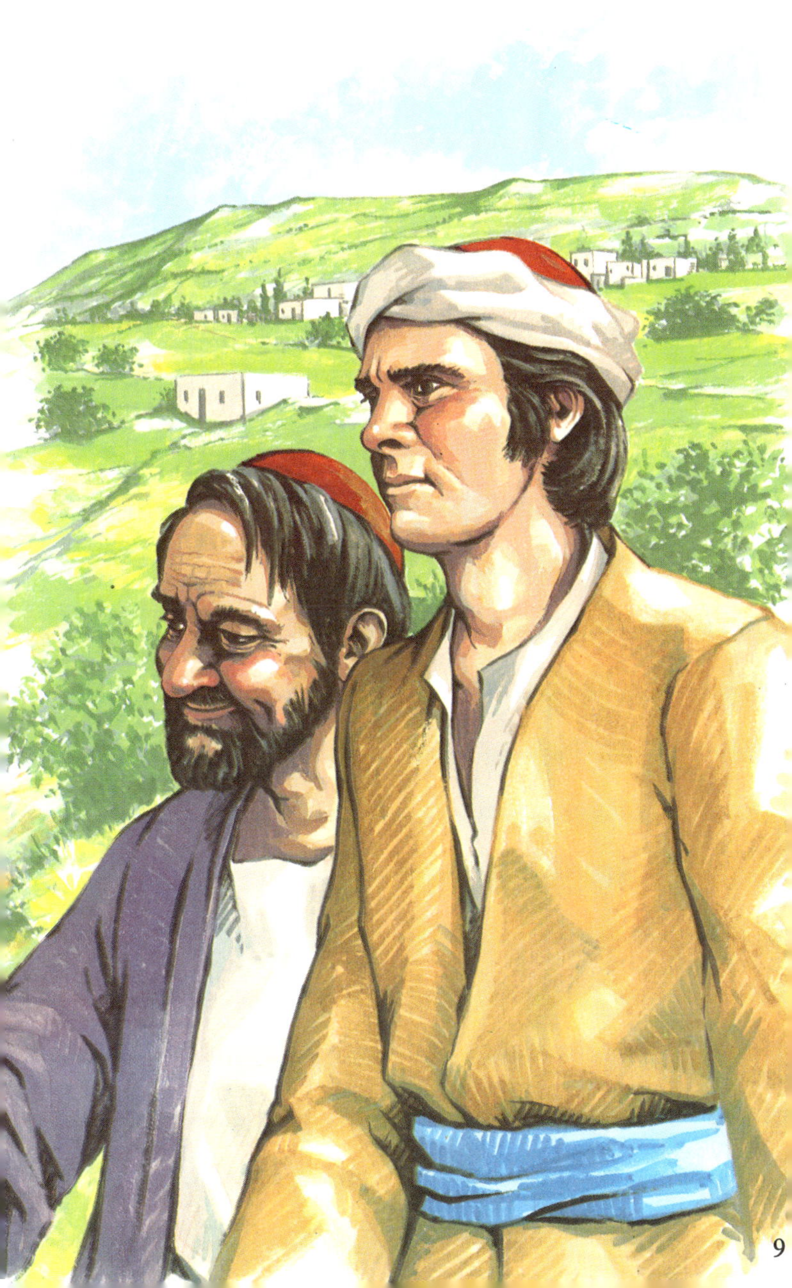

Just outside the town, the river flowed slowly through sandy fields. "The children would love a house here," thought Simeon. "It would be pleasant for my wife too, and the sand would be easy to dig—but not very firm to build on."

He walked on until he came to a place where the river flowed through rocky banks.

"This is the place for our house," Simeon decided. "It may be a long walk from town, but the rock will be firm to build on, and safer than sand."

He went back to the farmer and bought part of the rocky field.

When he got home, he told his wife all about it.

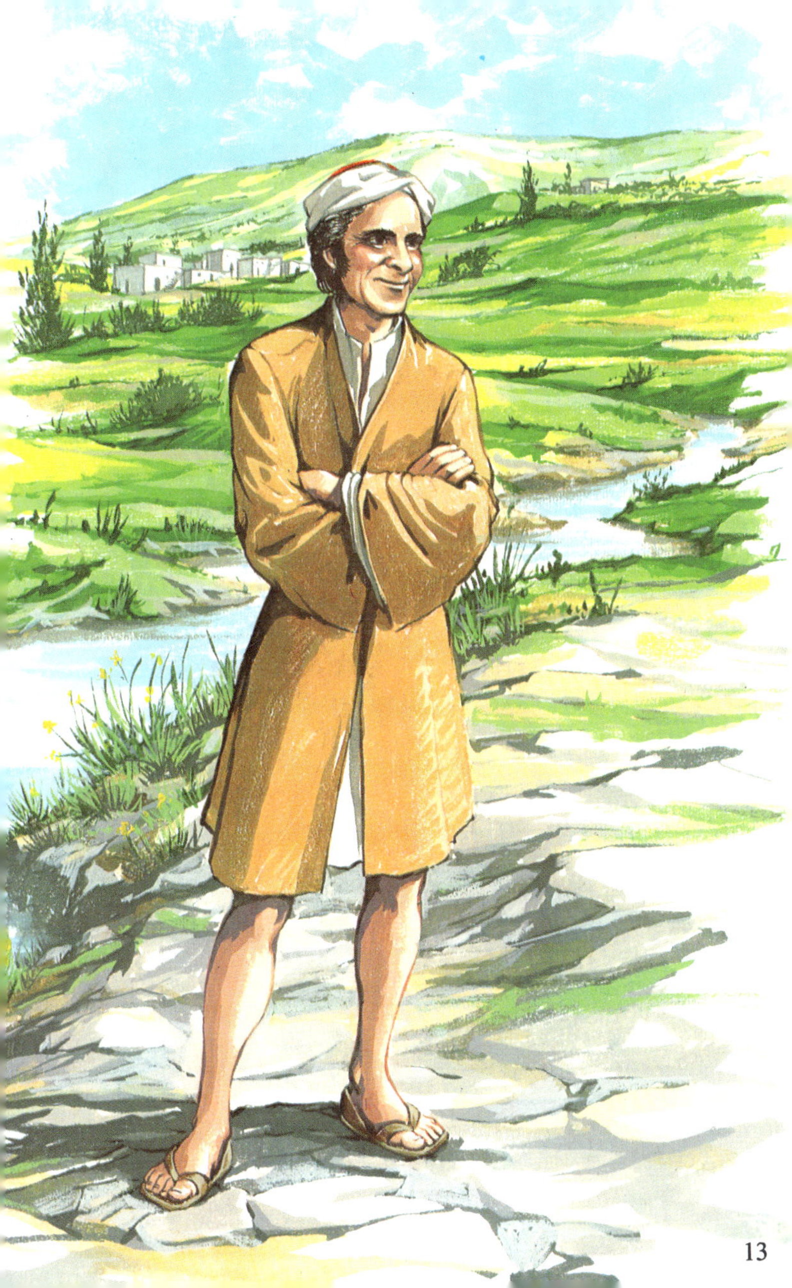

"Wouldn't it be easier to build on the sand?" she said. "It would be nearer, and much easier to carry the bricks down there."

"I agree," said Simeon. "It would be much easier to build on the sand — but once the house is built, I want it to last. On the rock a house will be safe and dry. It may be more difficult to build, but worth the trouble."

15

The next day Simeon and his men began to build. It was a long way out to the rocky field with the bricks.

Each night when Simeon came home, he gathered his family for evening prayers.

They thanked God for the lovely site they had been able to buy, and for the hard work all the men were doing.

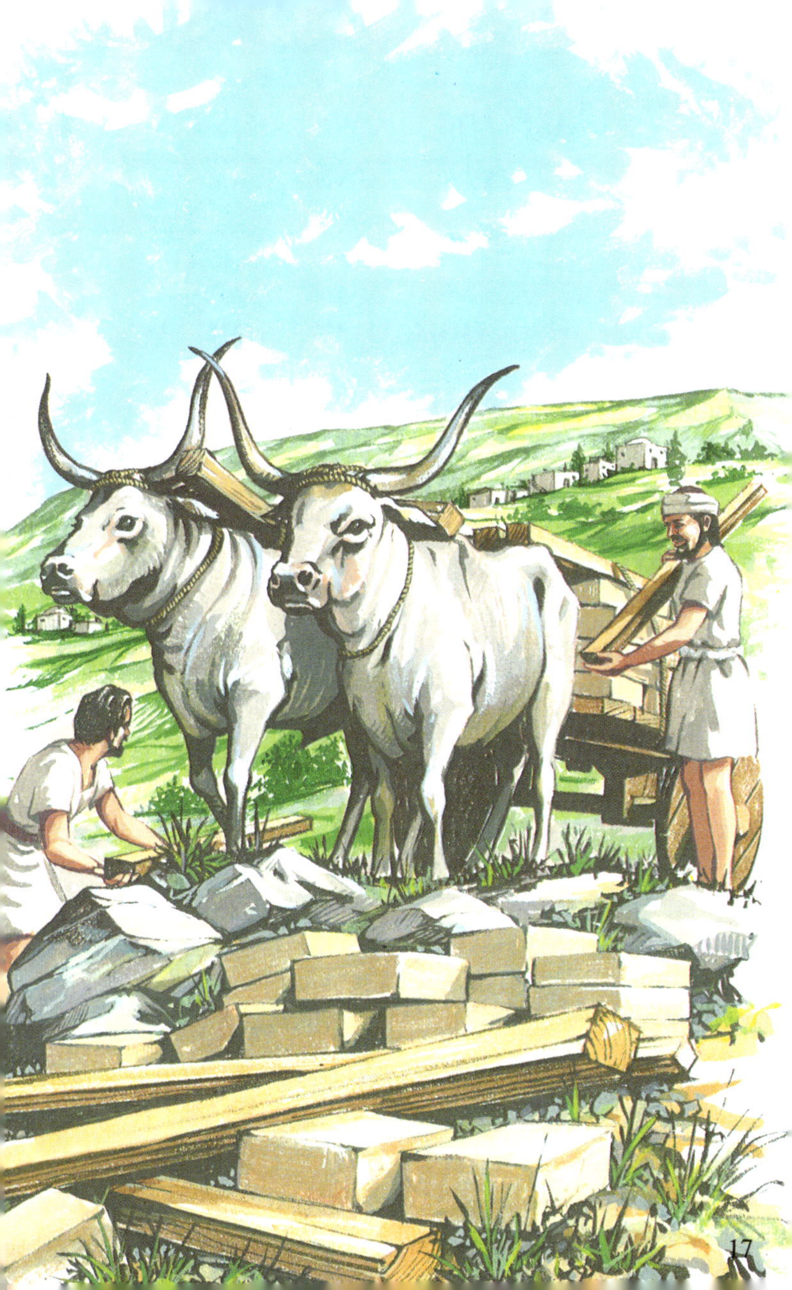

At last the new house was finished. How excited Simeon and his family were. As soon as the house had dried and was quite ready, they moved in.

They all helped to carry blankets, lamps, cooking pots, water jars and stores of food.

Soon the house looked cosy and warm with a light shining and everything neat and tidy.

19

The children found it hard to sleep that night, because they were so excited. Early in the morning they were up and out, picking wild flowers and playing among the rocks.

Soon the summer was over and winter came. It was a wet year and slowly the river rose higher and higher. Everyone was talking about it in the town.

Watching from their new house, Simeon's family grew alarmed as the river rose.

"What shall we do if the river floods?" asked Simeon's wife.

"Our house is strongly built," said Simeon, "and even if the river does flood it can't wash away this great rock we have built on."

That night there was a big storm. The wind howled and blew round the house, battering against it. The lightning flashed and the thunder rumbled overhead.

The rain poured down. No one could sleep and everyone got up.

"I'm scared the river will flood tonight," said Simeon's wife.

"We have prayed, and God will keep us safe," Simeon said bravely.

25

He went to the door and looked out into the dark night. Suddenly a flash of lightning lit up the sky. In that moment he saw the brown waters of the river burst over the banks and come rushing towards them.

A great wave of water swirled round the rock and lashed against it. A blast of wind swept down and shook the house.

Simeon came back to his family and spoke gently to them. "This house is built safely on a rock," he said. "The water cannot wash it away. The wind cannot blow it down. We are in God's hands, and we are safe. Go to sleep now."

As the night passed, the wind slowly died down. The rain stopped. The storm was over. The house was safe!

29

But not every house had stood up to the storm that night. Outside the town on the sandy field, another man called David had just built himself a new house too.

He had asked the farmer to sell him some land, just as Simeon had done. "Come with me," said the farmer. "I will show you what land I have got."

31

He took David to the rocky field first. He showed him how much land Simeon had bought, and showed him how much was left.

"It is a nice view here," said David, "but it is a long way from the town. Show me the rest of your land."

The farmer took David to the sandy field. David liked it at once.

33

"This is ideal," he said, as he looked round. "Water at hand, a flat surface, and easy soil to dig—my men can begin right away. Let me buy this field."

That same day David and his men began work. They soon piled up the wood and bricks they needed in the nearby sandy field.

Quite quickly the house began to rise. David's family used to come to see how the men were getting on.

Each night when David got home, he quickly ate his supper and went to bed. "I am too tired to pray," he said. "I will pray tomorrow."

At last David's house was finished.

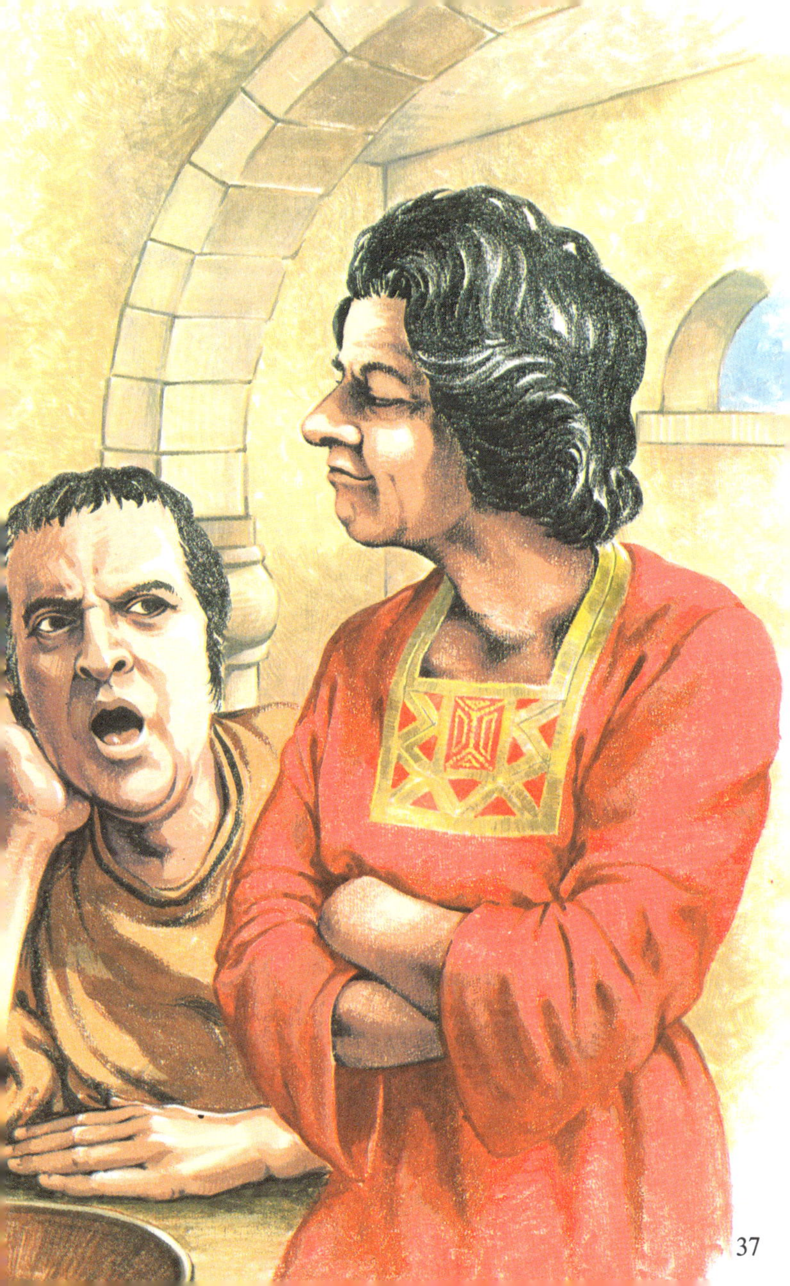

All the family were very excited when they moved into the new house. When they woke up on their first morning, they could hear the river running along nearby and the trees rustling overhead.

Soon the summer ended and winter came. When the river began to rise, David's wife grew very worried.

39

"If the river floods, will it reach us?" she asked.

"I hope not," said David. "We are not quite on the edge of the river. Even if the floods do come, our house will be safe. It is new and strong."

But on the night of the great storm there was alarm in David's family. The wind shook and rocked the house.

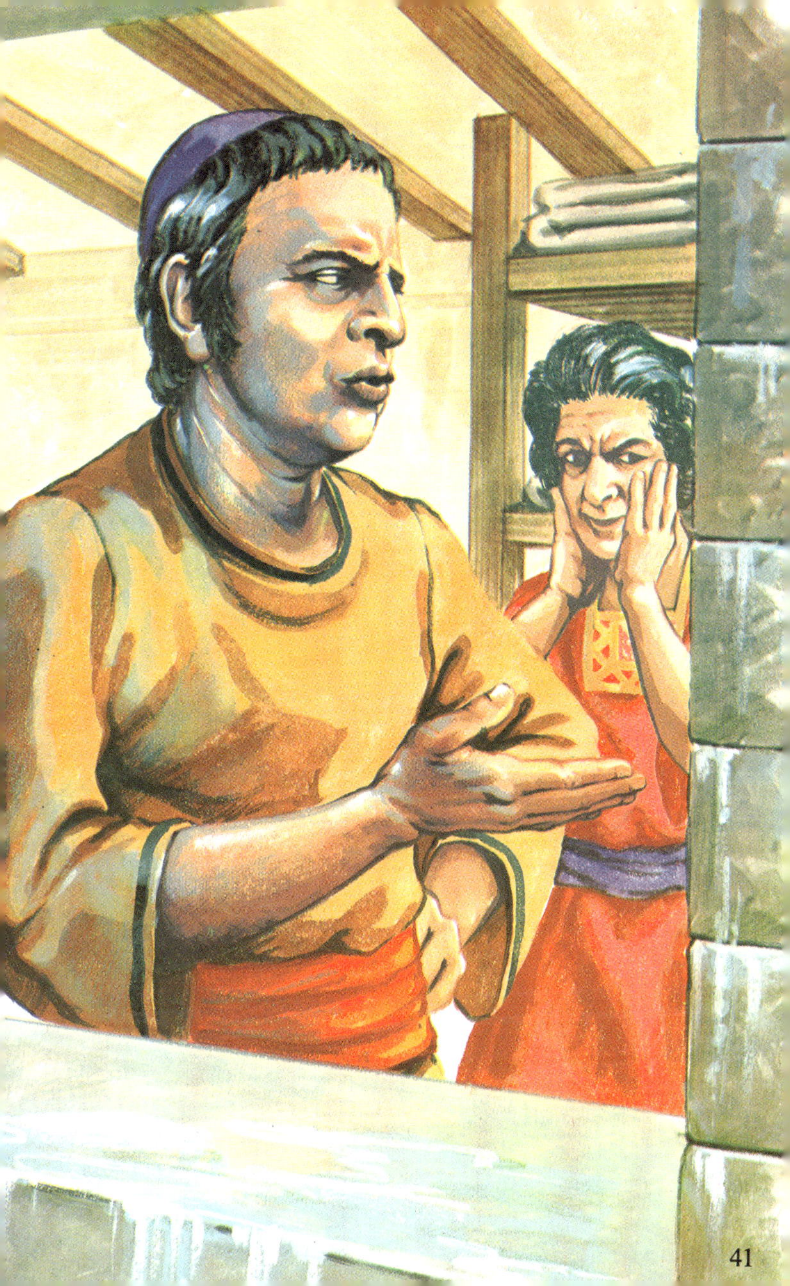

The rain beat down hard and began to wash away the sand from beneath the house.

Gradually some of the plaster was loosened. Bricks began to show. David's family were frightened by the thunder, the rain and the wind as it rattled the doors.

"We shall have the floods in here soon," wept David's wife.

43

They were so frightened that they did not look out of the house to see what was happening. None of them saw the river break over its banks and come rushing towards them.

With a sudden roar the floodwater reached the house.

"Quick! Everyone out!" cried David, as the water swirled under the door. "Get to higher ground."

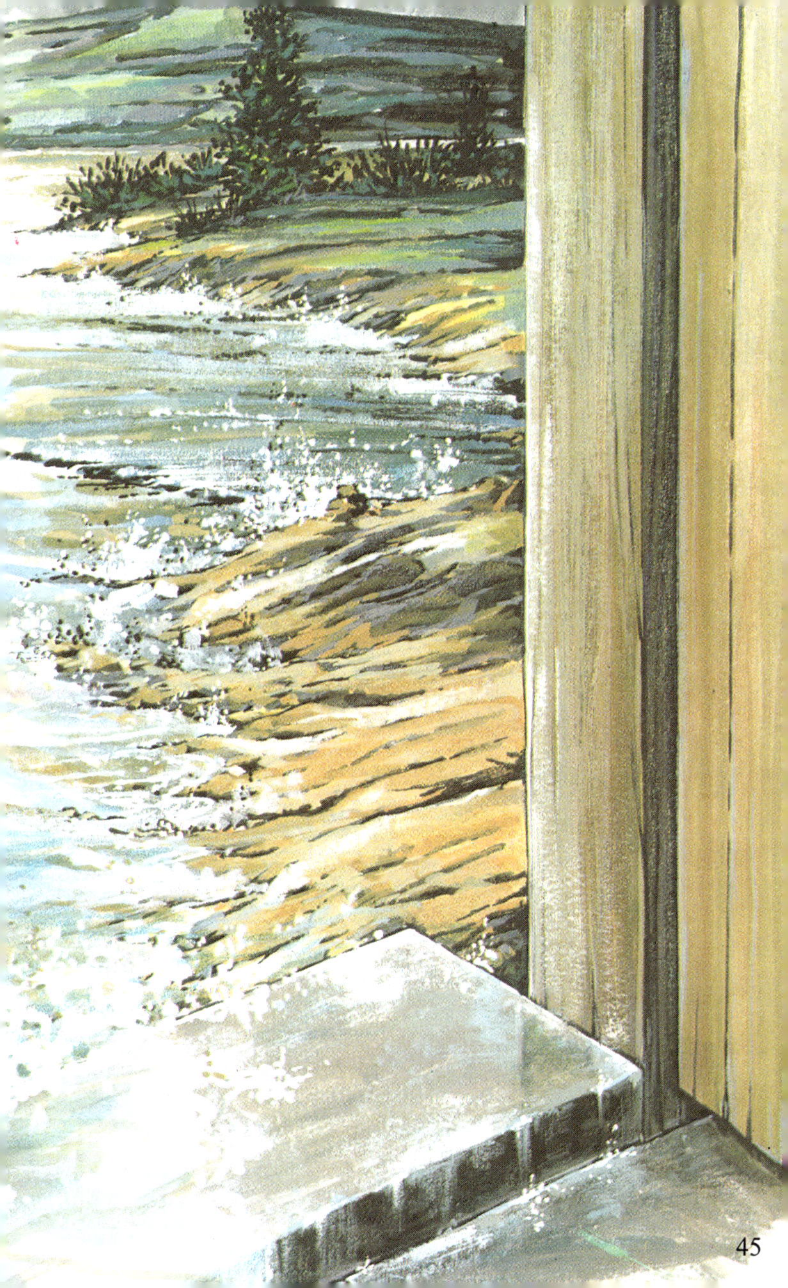

Hurrying as fast as they could through the water, the family escaped.

The flood washed away the sand from beneath the house. Loose bricks were swept away. In great blasts the wind shook the weakened walls.

With a loud roar, David's house suddenly fell to the ground. "Sand! Oh why did I build on the sand?" cried David in the dark.

Jesus says that those who listen to what He says, and obey Him, are building their lives wisely on rock.

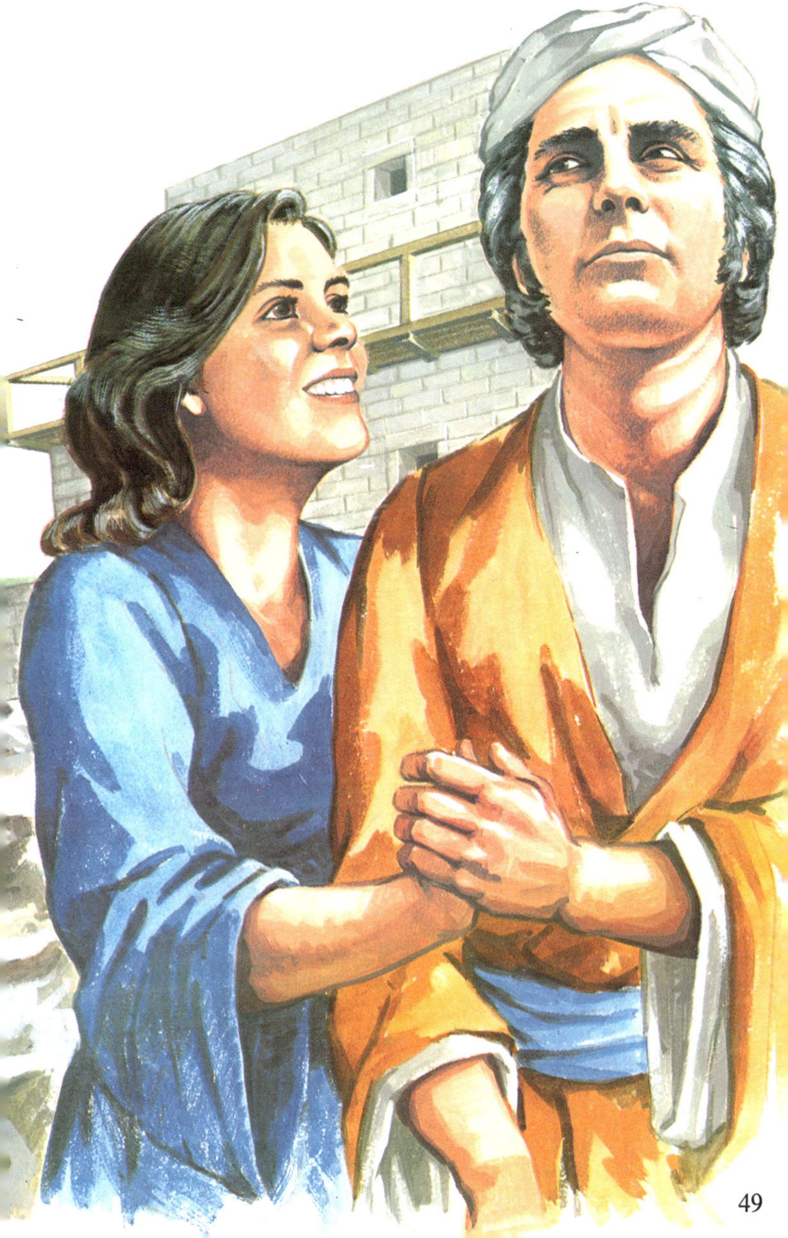

Those who listen to what Jesus says and take no notice, are building their lives foolishly on sand.

51